"Logan was a good player, but here the Vestige kids were on another level.

Dave Sands scored with an amazing overhead kick. Pete Chapman's passes were powerful and accurate. They never played like that at school.

What was the team's secret ingredient? 

FOOTBALL FORCE

Football Force
by Jonny Zucker
Illustrated by Bob Moulder

Published by Ransom Publishing Ltd.
Unit 7, Brocklands Farm, West Meon, Hampshire
GU32 1JN, UK
www.ransom.co.uk

ISBN 978 178127 713 3
First published in 2015
Reprinted 2015

Copyright © 2015 Ransom Publishing Ltd.
Text copyright © 2015 Jonny Zucker
Illustrations copyright © 2015 Bob Moulder

A CIP catalogue record of this book is available from the British Library.

All rights reserved. No part of this publication may be reproduced, stored in a retrieval system, or transmitted, in any form or by any means, electronic, mechanical, photocopying, recording or otherwise, without the prior permission of the publishers.

The rights of Jonny Zucker to be identified as the author and of Bob Moulder to be identified as the illustrator of this Work have been asserted by them in accordance with sections 77 and 78 of the Copyright, Design and Patents Act 1988.

Football Force

Jonny Zucker

Illustrated by

Bob Moulder

LEISURE AND CULTURE DUNDEE	
C00747445X	
Bertrams	01/06/2015
	£6.99
WHIT	

It's 2066.

A new material called Territe
has recently been invented.

Football players of all ages
have started wearing boots, shin pads
and elbow pads made from Territe.

It's tough and it's light.
It offers the body lots of protection.

People are calling it
Football Body Armour.

CHAPTER 1

SLAM!

The ball smashed into the back of the Melton Town net for the third time that afternoon.

Melton were the local youth team Logan Smith played for. They'd lost their last four matches.

The other team in town, Vestige United, were doing brilliantly. They were top of the league.

They'd scored loads of goals and had let in hardly any.

Logan didn't understand this.

Most of the players from both teams went to his school. He'd seen them play in the playground. He'd seen them play in the park.

The Vestige United players were no better than the Melton Town players in these places.

And yet, when it came to league matches, the Vestige crew were a million times better.

It was a total mystery.

*****

On Thursday night, Logan went to see Vestige United play Ivy City. They thrashed them 6-0.

They played fantastically. Their passing, shooting and dribbling were incredible. Their body strength was awesome.

What was their secret? Were their coaches amazing? Did they train in a special way that made OK players perform brilliantly in matches?

They all wore Territe boots, shin pads and elbow pads, but so did all the Melton players, including Logan.

So it couldn't be that.

Logan was desperate to find out what Vestige's secret was. He was also keen to play for a successful team.

Football wasn't so much fun when you lost every game.

After a quick internet search, Logan found the phone number of Vestige United's assistant manager, Kevin Reed.

He dialled the number.

'Hello,' said a voice. 'Kevin Reed here.'

'Er … hello. I'd like to try out for Vestige United. Are you looking for players?' asked Logan.

'Yes we are,' said Reed. 'Give me your details and then come over for a trial. How about Monday afternoon at 4.30 p.m.? Do you know where our training ground is?'

Smiling, Logan said he knew the ground. He'd be there at 4.30.

CHAPTER 2

Logan went straight to the Vestige United training ground after school on Monday.

It was a large rectangle of grass that stood behind some disused garages. There was a changing room standing near an old, run-down brown hut.

Logan was surprised to find all of the Vestige players already changed into their kit.

They were wearing their Territe boots, shin pads and elbow pads, plus blue Vestige United Shirts with a large white dove crest on the chest and white Vestige shorts.

Kevin Reed was there to greet Logan.

'Nice to meet you,' smiled Reed. 'Good luck today.'

He gave Logan a Vestige United shirt and shorts. For some reason, the shirt didn't have the dove crest.

'Get these on,' said Reed.

Logan hurried inside the changing room, put on the shirt and shorts and shoved his

clothes and trainers into one of the grey lockers.

He slid on his Territe elbow and shin pads and laced up his red Territe boots.

Trotting out onto the grass, he recognised a couple of lads from his school – Dave Sands and Pete Chapman. They both gave him quick nods.

The Vestige United manager, Gary Tate, took training. Logan looked around for Kevin Reed, but he was nowhere to be seen.

To start, Tate had the players running round the pitch ten times. The Vestige players seemed to find this easy, but Logan struggled a bit.

This was baffling.

He was as fit as any Vestige player, yet here on the training ground they seemed to have bundles more energy.

Then they worked on passing and dribbling, followed by a mini match.

Logan was a good player, but here the Vestige kids were on another level.

Dave Sands scored with an amazing overhead kick. Pete Chapman's passes were powerful and accurate.

They never played like that at school.

But nothing that Gary Tate said or did seemed to be any different from what the Melton Town coaches said or did.

What was Tate's secret ingredient?

'OK, Logan,' said Reed, appearing after an hour. 'Go and get changed.'

While the others carried on training, Logan went back to the changing room, wondering if he'd done enough in his trial to get a place in the Vestige squad.

Considering he'd been the slowest and the least skilful, he thought it unlikely.

Logan changed out of his kit and then, making sure no one was around, started looking in the other kids' lockers.

Maybe the Vestige players drank some special sports drink that made them perform so well.

He was rummaging through one of the lockers when a deep male voice snarled: 'WHAT ON EARTH DO YOU THINK YOU'RE DOING?'

CHAPTER 3

Logan spun round.

Gary Tate was standing in the room, looking furious.

'Sorry Mr Tate, I er … I couldn't remember which locker I used. I was just trying to find my stuff.'

'Don't lie to me!' snarled Tate.

At that moment, Kevin Reed stuck his head round the changing room door.

'What's all the shouting about?' he asked.

'This trial kid was looking in other people's lockers,' snarled Tate. 'I said we shouldn't give trials to anyone new!'

'Relax,' smiled Reed. 'He was probably looking for his stuff.'

'That's exactly what I told Mr Tate,' said Logan, with relief.

'Go easy, Gary,' said Reed in a firm voice. 'You know what the league said about us not taking on any new players. We have to take at least one, or they'll start hassling us. I say we take him.'

Logan was amazed. Why did Reed want to let him in when he was clearly nowhere as good as the others – at least in training?

Tate scowled at Reed for a few moments and then, muttering under his breath, he stormed out of the changing room.

'Thanks Mr Reed,' grinned Logan.

'Training starts tomorrow at 4.30 p.m., and we train every day of the week,' said Reed.

'We train our players hard, Logan. Get here at 4 p.m. sharp. The shirt and shorts I gave you are now yours.'

Logan was about to say that his shirt didn't have the dove crest like the others, but he stopped himself.

You probably had to 'earn' the club shirt and he definitely hadn't done that today.

'Sounds great,' nodded Logan. 'See you tomorrow.' He was in!

Reed left and Logan put his kit in his bag.

As he walked outside he could see Gary Tate still putting the Vestige gang through their paces.

If anything, the players were playing even better than before. What exactly was going on here?

But hang on a minute, he reminded himself. *I'm one of them now. I'm going to get a chance to see the Vestige training methods up close.*

And hopefully I'll become a far better player.

And with that thought buzzing around his brain, he hurried home in a fine mood.

CHAPTER 4

The following day, Logan turned up at the Vestige United training ground at 3.50 p.m.

He was amazed to see the Vestige players already changed and out on the pitch kicking balls around.

Logan went up to Kevin Reed. 'I thought you said to be here by four?'

'I did,' nodded Reed, 'the others are just ultra-keen.'

Once again, during training Reed was nowhere to be seen, while Gary Tate pushed the players to do loads of running, press-ups, sit-ups and stretches.

In a session of 'Keepy-Uppy' Logan was in a three with Pete Chapman and Dave Sands. Logan did well, but Pete and Dave were sensational.

However, once again, there were no magical coaching tips.

And then a thought hit Logan. Maybe the shin pads, elbow pads and boots the Vestige players wore were made of a special, new kind of Territe.

He needed to find out.

When a four-a-side game started, Logan did a well-timed sliding tackle on Pete Chapman.

As they fell into a heap on the floor, Logan grabbed onto one of Pete's boots and shin pads and squeezed them.

They felt exactly the same as his pads and boots. Both were Territe, plain and simple.

It looked like the secret didn't lie in Vestige's Territe gear.

*****

Once again, Logan was sent off to change before the others.

'All new players change first,' explained Reed.

Logan left training that afternoon feeling frustrated. Maybe there was nothing going on at Vestige.

Maybe the players just tried much, much harder for Vestige United than they did at school or in the park.

Or maybe, just maybe, he'd been fooling himself and he was nowhere near as good as they were.

CHAPTER 5

On Wednesday afternoon, Gary Tate made an announcement during training.

'As you all know, we are playing Root City in the Youth Cup Final this Saturday. The prize is a big sponsorship deal with Croydens – the electrical company.'

Everyone nodded.

'Well, I know it's last minute, but we've just been told that the game will now be taking place at the Emirates Stadium – Arsenal's home ground.'

'YES!' shouted all of the players, including Logan.

This was incredible news.

'The game will last fifteen minutes,' said Reed. 'We'll play it during half-time in the Arsenal v Liverpool match.'

*****

Everyone trained extra hard that afternoon. They all wanted to impress Tate and make it into the team for Saturday's game at the Emirates.

Tate shouted at Logan a couple of times and criticised some of his passes.

But still, no matter how much effort Logan put in, everyone else was miles better than him.

'Don't worry if you don't make the team for a while,' said Reed to Logan, when he appeared after training. 'I'm sure you'll get there.'

Logan frowned. Why did Gary Tate have to be so horrible to him, and yet Kevin Reed encouraged him? It was like they were working for two different teams.

Logan went to change first as usual, but then, instead of going home, he went round the back of the changing room and waited.

*****

It was a while before Reed and the other players finally left. As Logan waited, he saw

Gary Tate come out of the changing room and make a call on his mobile.

'Are the supplies ready?' Tate said into the mouthpiece. He listened for the answer.

'And the connections are all clean?' he asked. A pause.

'Excellent,' he said. 'See you then.'

Tate killed the call and started walking towards the road at a brisk pace.

Logan waited a few seconds and then began to follow him.

CHAPTER 6

As Logan followed Tate, questions raced through his mind.

What had he meant by '*Are the connections clean?*'

Were these connections with other clubs? Was it something to do with betting and match fixing? He'd read something about that kind of thing in the paper.

*****

Twenty minutes later, Logan watched Tate enter an old lock-up unit on a back road near town.

Hiding behind an old truck, Logan could see a young guy with a beard and big sideburns handing Tate a packet. Tate looked at its contents, stuffed it into his bag and walked out.

Logan was sure Tate hadn't seen him.

He waited until Tate had gone and then started to walk back into town. He'd gone less than fifty metres when he bumped into someone.

It was Kevin Reed.

'Hey Logan,' said Reed. 'What are you doing round here?'

'I, erm, I had to pick up some sugar for my mum,' lied Logan, pointing to the small supermarket on the other side of the road.

Logan made a snap decision to ask Reed what was going on.

'Kevin,' he began. 'Is something weird happening at Vestige United?'

'What do you mean?' frowned Reed.

'I'm not sure. The players just seem to play miles better for the team than they do at school. What makes them so good?'

'It's all down to Gary Tate,' smiled Reed. 'They play extra hard because they're terrified of him.'

Logan pulled a face. Could being scared of your manager really make you that much better?

He wasn't convinced.

What he was convinced of was that something weird had to be going on at Vestige United. He didn't know what it was, but he reckoned it was connected to the package Tate had just collected.

Kevin Reed was a good guy, but it sounded like he had no idea what was going on.

After all, Tate took all of the training sessions while Reed scooted off somewhere.

Whatever dodgy things were going on at Vestige United, it was Gary Tate who was leading them.

As Logan walked home, he felt more determined than ever to get to the bottom of the mystery.

CHAPTER 7

On Thursday, Logan turned up at the training ground at 3.30 p.m. No one was around. The changing room was locked.

A few minutes later Gary Tate arrived. He was carrying the bag the bearded guy had given him the day before.

Tate had a quick look to check the coast was clear and then went round to the back of the battered hut next to the changing room.

Logan frowned. Why was he going there?

Logan followed and watched Tate punch some numbers into an entry panel at the side of the door. There was a click, and the door opened.

Tate went inside and shut the door. He was in there for a good five minutes.

When he finally emerged he had a large grin on his face.

Logan waited until Tate went off to open up the changing room. Then he slunk over to the back door of the battered hut.

He'd seen the numbers Tate had punched into the keypad, so he entered them in the same sequence. There was a click and the door opened.

Logan stepped inside and closed the door behind him. He stopped abruptly, astonished by what he saw.

Inside the hut there were several tables. On the tables were hundreds of wires and electronics, and a pile of neatly stacked Vestige United blue dove crests.

There were also stacks of diagrams and charts.

Logan quickly pulled out his mobile and started taking pictures.

He hadn't been in there for more than a couple of minutes when he heard a chilling sound.

Numbers on the security panel were being punched in.

Then there was a click, and the door opened.

CHAPTER 8

Gary Tate came into the room. He'd left his wallet in the hut and had come back for it.

If he'd looked down, even for a fraction of a second, he would have seen Logan crouching beneath one of the tables.

But Tate didn't look down. He saw his wallet on a chair, picked it up and quickly walked out of the hut.

OK, thought Logan. *Now I have a pretty good idea what's going on. I have to tell someone. And I reckon Kevin Reed is the person to tell. He'll help me.*

Throughout the training session that morning, Logan kept looking around for Kevin Reed. But there was no sign of him.

Nor did Reed show up when Tate called training to a close.

*****

Training on Friday was short and sharp. Logan was nervous – he felt something big was about to go down and he wanted to put a stop to it.

But he'd have to be very, very careful. Having Gary Tate as an enemy was a pretty frightening thought.

'Right,' said Tate when training was over. 'I want everyone at the Emirates Stadium at 2 p.m. tomorrow. Here are the security passes that will get you inside the building.

'Logan, you're getting a ticket to come and see the game. You're not ready to play for us yet.'

Logan had been expecting something like this, but he still felt disappointed.

*****

At 1.30 p.m. on Saturday, Logan arrived at the Emirates. Loads of Arsenal and Liverpool fans were milling around, talking and joking.

STADIUM

Logan went through one of the turnstiles and walked up a flight of stairs. If, as he suspected, Tate was up to secret, dodgy tactics here at the Emirates, Logan was going to find out what they were.

Seeing a door marked PRIVATE, Logan pushed at it.

It opened.

He walked through and found himself in a long corridor. He hurried along and entered another corridor. He tried two doors, one on either side of the corridor.

They were both locked.

He turned another corner and that was when he spotted Kevin Reed.

'KEVIN!' he shouted with relief. At last he could let Reed know what was going on.

Kevin turned round.

'Logan?' he said with a puzzled expression. 'How did you get in here?'

'That doesn't matter,' replied Logan. 'You've got to help me, Kevin. Gary Tate is up to something really bad – I'm sure of it. He's cheating in some way and I have a pretty good idea what … '

But before Logan could finish his sentence, Kevin opened a door in the corridor marked STOREROOM.

He shoved Logan inside the room, slammed the door and locked him in.

CHAPTER 9

'HEY!' yelled Logan, banging on the door, 'LET ME OUT!'

He heard Reed's footsteps hurrying away.

Logan could have kicked himself. Kevin Reed must be in on it too! And now Reed had locked Logan in this storeroom, with a few old Arsenal posters on the wall and nothing else.

Vestige United would win the match and Tate and Reed would get their hands on all of that sponsorship money.

That must be why they were doing this. They were complete crooks.

And even if Logan was let out after the game, and if he told people – Tate and Reed would just say he was a stupid kid making up stories. It would be his word against theirs.

Logan tried the door and windows. All firmly locked. He banged on the door again, but nobody came.

He paced round the room for ages. He checked his watch. It was 2.30 p.m.

At 3 p.m. he heard a giant roar as the Arsenal v Liverpool match kicked off. At 3.20 p.m. there was massive cheering. Arsenal must have scored.

3.30 p.m. arrived. In fifteen minutes it would be half time and the Vestige United game would begin.

In anger and frustration, Logan ripped one of the old Arsenal posters off the wall. Behind it was a mesh metal grate. He pulled at it. It came away easily. Behind it was a short passage that led back into the corridor.

Result!

Logan scrambled through the passage and entered the corridor.

He checked his watch. It was 3.40.

21A
STEWARD

He ran forward and reached a large area where drinks and snacks were being sold. There weren't too many people around, because there were still five minutes of play before half time.

Logan went straight up to the nearest steward.

'Can you take me to the stadium announcer please?' he asked.

'Is it an emergency?' asked the steward.

'Without question,' replied Logan in a very determined voice.

CHAPTER 10

On the Emirates pitch, the Vestige United v Root City game had been going for five minutes.

It was already 2-0 to Vestige. Pete Chapman had scored with an unbelievably powerful shot. Then Dave Sands had dived to score an impossible-looking header.

Suddenly the stadium announcer spoke out over the speakers.

'We need to interrupt this game for a very important announcement.'

The players stopped where they were.

'It has come to our attention that Vestige United are not playing fairly.'

On the giant Emirates screens flashed up images of the Vestige blue dove team crest, which Logan had photographed in the old hut. He'd opened one up, and the next picture on the screens showed a large microchip at its centre.

The crowd gasped.

Diagrams then appeared on the screens showing Vestige United's boots, shin pads and elbow pads.

These contained tiny embedded electrodes that were connected to the crest microchip.

They allowed the Vestige players to run impossibly fast, make gigantic leaps and carry out extra-crunching tackles.

That was why Logan had been made to change before the other players.

If he'd seen a shirt lying around and had studied the crest, he might have spotted the microchip and worked out that the Vestige players were getting a very unfair advantage.

Next, the screens showed Gary Tate, down on the pitch. He was standing on the touchline, looking ashen-faced.

But it wasn't him controlling his players. The screens panned round the stadium and picked out Kevin Reed.

He was crouched behind a low wall, hunched over a laptop. Obviously he was operating all of the players' chips and electrodes – making them perform ten times better than their natural skill and pace would let them.

That was why Reed was never at training. He was out of sight, operating the players.

Hisses and shouts of fury rang out round the stadium as the Vestige United players were escorted off the field.

Police officers grabbed Reed and Tate and led them away.

The picture on the giant screen then cut to adverts.

'Well done!' said the stadium announcer to Logan, handing him a card.

'What's that?' asked Logan.

'You've got your own box for the second half,' grinned the announcer. 'I think such great detective work deserves a prize. Are you up for it?'

But Logan was already running out of the room, clutching the card.

Forget improving his football skills.

Forget the disgraced Vestige United coaches and players.

He had a box at the Emirates.

And there was a whole second half to watch!

TOXIC

Now read the first chapter of another great Toxic title by Jonny Zucker:

THE BATTLE OF THE UNDERSEA KINGDOM

CHAPTER 1

'The mayor has been kidnapped!' screeched an elderly woman, as she ran into the sea-front boat repair shop.

Danny and his dad, Tyler, looked up from the boat they were fixing and followed the woman out of the shop.

It was dusk, and the sleepy little village of Tidehaven should have been quiet.

But now everyone was gathered in the village square.

A village elder called Caleb was holding up a piece of paper.

'We found this ransom note,' he explained. 'It says we will only get the mayor back if we pay a hundred gold coins to his kidnappers.'

'Where was the note found?' shouted someone.

'On the beach,' replied Caleb.

'The kidnappers must come from a nearby village,' said someone else.

'They want the money to be left on the rocks, by the sand dunes at the top end of the village,' said Caleb.

'Which village do you think did it?' asked someone.

'You are all wrong!' said Tyler in a loud, clear voice.

Everyone fell silent.

'The kidnappers do not come from another village. They come from under the sea.'

'This is no time for your silly sea stories, Tyler,' said Caleb wearily.

Everybody knew about Tyler and his strange stories about creatures under the sea.

Nobody took him seriously – they all just thought he was a bit odd.

'The note was found on the beach,' continued Tyler. 'The ransom money is to be left near the sand dunes. Sea creatures are the kidnappers – it's obvious.'

But Tyler was shouted down. The villagers ignored him and carried on talking about other villages.

Tyler and Danny listened to the other villagers for a while. Then they returned to their repair shop.

'Get some sleep son,' said Tyler. 'We have much work to do.'

Danny nodded. He didn't know if his dad's stories about creatures under the sea were true or not, and he had no idea what his dad was planning.

But there was no way he was going to miss it.

More Great Toxic Reads

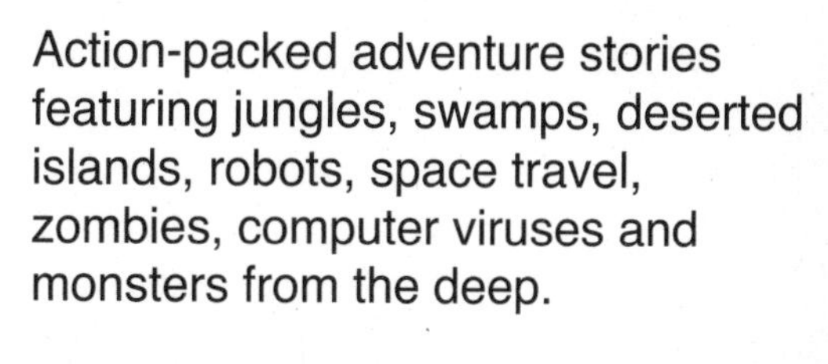

Action-packed adventure stories featuring jungles, swamps, deserted islands, robots, space travel, zombies, computer viruses and monsters from the deep.

How many have you read?

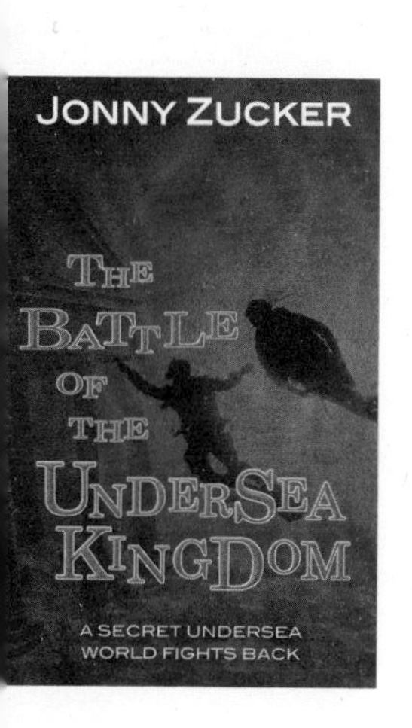

The Battle of the Undersea Kingdom

by Jonny Zucker

When the local mayor is kidnapped, the people suspect other villages of taking him. But Danny's dad, Tyler, knows more. He thinks that creatures from under the sea are to blame – and he's going to prove it!

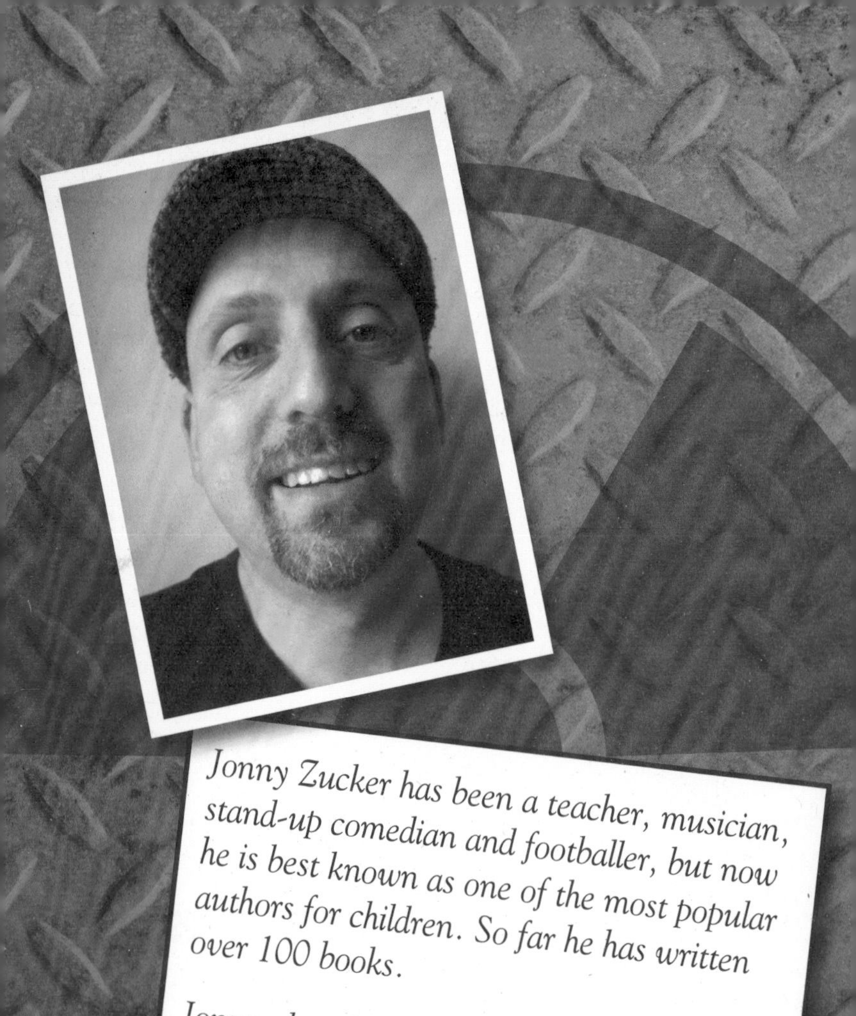

Jonny Zucker has been a teacher, musician, stand-up comedian and footballer, but now he is best known as one of the most popular authors for children. So far he has written over 100 books.

Jonny also plays in a band and has done over 60 gigs as a stand-up comedian, reaching the London Region Final of the BBC New Comedy awards.

He still dreams of being a professional footballer.